First Edition

Published in the UK, USA & Europe by
Max Publsihing

ISBN 9798758327609

shame shames
and other stories

max scratchmann

Max Publishing

max scratchmann

contents

5

max scratchmann

"At Chandrapore the Turtons were little gods; but soon
they would retire to some suburban villa,
and die exiled from glory."

E M Forster
A Passage to India

max scratchmann

shame-shames

S he sits nervously in the lounge of the house that she must now learn to call her own, though it still feels too large, too loose, like wearing Mumma's shoes when she was a babe playing dress-up. Outside, the afternoon sun bounces off the dusty drive and wafts the hothouse scent of the pseudo-English gardens that the *maalees* have laboriously watered this morning, blood-red dahlias wilting in the late May heat, everyone praying for the rains which are, as usual, late in coming.

The Burrah Memsahib has, of course, chosen a suitably inconvenient hour of the day to make her introductory visit, when the men are all abed before facing the heat and dust of the mill again, and the servant sits sullenly in the kitchen with sandwiches sweltering under a damp dish cloth, ready to make tea, resenting having been forbidden his *charpoy* at an hour when all sane souls are comatose. Method in the Memsahib's madness, no doubt, for at this hour so very few will see her arrive at what may turn out to be a House of Shame.

Patsy rises with difficulty and looks at herself in the big mirror, the one that had stood in his grandmother's house and her mother's before her, he had told her proudly. Just like the clock on the sideboard which would chime sonorously in a few short minutes, its ding-dong-ding-

9

dong reminding him of Home, he said. Though the school teacher had said that the old clock made the chimes of the Big Ben in London and Her Fergus was from a tiny village in the north of Ireland, and had never been to the Englishmen's capital city in his short life as far as she knew.

Oh, Ireland, she had gushed to him while he waltzed with her in the ballroom that night under a waxy Calcutta moon. *My Mumma's Mumma came from...* She searched for the name from her old convent school geography book. *...Donegal. Dear old Donegal,* she added for good measure, though it didn't matter either way, he was already besotted.

And today, standing before his mirror like a victorious swimmer on the gold-medalist's block, her belly plump with the coming baby, she feels sulky rather than triumphant, still resenting those Armenian girls from her high school classes who boasted naturally creamy-coloured skin and passed easily for white. *Oh yes, our family comes from the Home Counties originally,* they lied shamefacedly to gauche tea-planters' sons in town for the weekend. *Though, of course, we've always lived here because of Daddy's business interests. I'd love for someone who knows the ropes to show me the sights of Home...*

The sights of Home, indeed... Girls like that have never really had to try, she pouts, flopping back into her chair, and even at convent school it had been a constant battle, keeping her pinafore as clean as the English girls', angling her little white socks just like theirs and being ever-so good-mannered when they took her back home to their man-sions for tea and inquisitions from stony-faced Memsahibs in starched print frocks. Watching her table graces like beady-eyed hawks, suspicious of this cuckoo their golden-haired children had introduced into their colonial nests. Always alert for some slip; while she, feral creature that she is, her head inclined, nostrils sniffing the wind, sits listening for some subtle clue, some indication that the Mummies have "asked around" and will abruptly withdraw invitations to birthday celebrations on their riverside lawns, her lacy party dress hung back in the armoire, Mumma's skilful hands letting it out again each season so that it would last and last. No money for a new one as she grew now that there was no longer work for Mumma, not when the English ladies whispered together and discovered What Had Happened sixteen years before. The fair-skinned sahib with hair the colour of the sly foxes in her kindergarten ABC book, the one who was ever so nice to his children's pretty kohl-eyed ayah before the Scene With the Wife and the flight in the night to their new rooms in Chowringhee, two hundred rupees in a plain envelope on the first of each month. But what would happen when the sahib was posted back to England and the payments ceased, what then? *I'm relying on you, daughter.* Stay out of the hot sun, keep your skin fair. Never, ever, wear native clothes, no gold in your ears and, god forbid, never your nose, always pretty dresses, full skirts and tight bodices like the peaches and cream girls wear. Always watch them, read their books, know their stories, see how they speak, pronounce. Copy their chatter. Be like them.

Copy cat, killed a rat, sitting on the butcher's hat, eating all the dirty fat…

11

Then along came Fergus, far from home in a strange world of sights and aromas and in love with this dark-eyed girl who had a grandmother in Donegal. *Dear old Donegal.* She had let him kiss her. Touch. Gone shame-shame with him in a hotel room one Saturday night and taken off her best dress before he ripped it. Let him do what he wanted. Though she had been shame-shame with English subalterns on weekend passes before, but those times she had kept her little white panties on and her butter-coloured thighs firmly shut tight, no hasty trips to the medicine woman before early morning trains to cantonments took sunburnt boys back to their barracks with whisky-tales to tell. *I met this totally fabulous Anglo-Indian girl on my Calcutta furlough, you know, very accommodating, if you know what I mean…*

Oh yes, shame-shame was all very well if it got you results, like the time when Mumma was so ill and the man from Benares had come with his camera, a friend of Aunty, he had claimed. *I can help in your hour of great need, Little Missy,* he'd said, his face locked in an avuncular smile, the red *sindura* on his forehead gleaming like an imitation ruby worn by black-faced sultans in the Ealing pictures she and Mumma used to avidly watch at the Metro in Chowringhee Road, a bright and alien thing in the semi dark of the sick room. *Please be accepting of my guarantee,* he had promised, a bead of sweat on his cheek, running down his neck to the collar and tie that he was not accustomed to wearing. *My discretion is absolute, none of these works of art will ever be seen in Calcutta, you have my word, I am not to be sullying your reputation.* Though she still worried in the small sleepless hours that someone would be on a trip and buy a little souvenir in a pale cream envelope, and see… But Mumma had been so very ill and the man had offered two hundred rupees. Though she had bargained for five and eventually settled on three. Three hundred rupees to go shame-shame for his camera. Not what a respectable Englishman's daughter would do, surely? But then…

Shame-shame, puppa-chame, all the other girls know your name…

And at first she had held out with Fergus but she knew it was what it would take to finally topple him over, tip the scales in her favour, seal the deal. Override the hostile looks of his servants when he brought her back to his house after their hasty wedding when she told him that there was a baby on the way. He, gallant, still remembering the blood from when they did the thing, she trying not to cry because it hurt her so, all grist to her mill, as the Sisters at her convent school would have said.

No, Fergus Dear, Mumma is too ill to come to the wedding, but you can meet her soon. Meet her after the baby is born and there's no going back, no hurried flights in the night to seedy rooms in back streets, stealthy envelops of hush money pushed under the door once a month. No meeting with Mumma who is black, black, black; your own little darkie-darkie servant woman who still likes to sit cross-legged on the floor and chew *paan* when she thinks she is alone. Mumma spent her life combing and preening English Memsahibs' little darlings, washing and dressing

13

them and pulling up their pretty socks. Dada might have been an English fox but wily Mumma outfoxed them all, bred her own little English - sorry, *Irish*, remember dear old Donegal - cuckoo and planted her right in your clean white nests. Oh yes, the fox's bastard daughter is a Memsahib now, and don't you forget it, here in the heat and dust of Rajnapor compounds or back in your Merry Sherwood Forests of Home.

The baby gives a little kick as she rises and walks slowly to the front hallway, her big belly heavy in the afternoon heat as the old clock chimes the hour. Time for the new Mrs Fergus McGinnlay to meet the Burrah Memsahib. Time to seal her fate…

bold as brass

It was in the insufferably hot months of the year that Lee Harvey Oswald shot the American president that the ladies of the Rajnapor Caledonian Society decided that it was time to finally do something about George Duncan.

They're saying that there's a child now, and that he sits in front of her house and openly plays with it, they whispered together over Whisky Sours at the club, sitting poolside under the hot-canvas smell of the big umbrellas that somehow gave the impression of being imported from distant seasides, though, in truth, they had known no other life than the Rajnapor Club and its environs. *And the inside of his house is a shambles, he's dismissed the sweeper and the bearer and only kept the cook so that no-one respectable can possibly visit...*

You don't think he actually allows her inside his house, do you? someone whispers.

*No, surely not, not even **he** would stoop so low,* they say. *Would he?* Looking to each other for reassurance. *They say that he sneaks over to her village after dark like a chicken-stealing fox, but of course all the workers recognise him in the moonlight and he even greets them if they meet, bold as brass...*

❖

She was seasick nearly the whole time on the long journey and paced the upper levels of the ship away from the smells of food and suntan oil and the crowds of returning memsahibs packing boarding school trunks and sulky children into crowded staterooms on the lower decks. There were flights available, of course, but the tickets were much more expensive and her aunt had limited resources.

Most days, she would pass the ship's nanny without acknowledgment around four-thirty, a tall austere woman still immaculate in her starched white uniform after a day of placating recalcitrant toddlers and screaming babes, taking her break before fussing matrons deposited their charges in anticipation of the seven o'clock dinner gong.

They used to call you the fishing fleet, the woman said out of the blue one pink-tinged evening, well into the voyage when Gibraltar was but a memory and Aden sat on the morning's horizon with its fleets of small boats ready to tempt bored children with tin toys and their mothers with cheap Japanese-made finery.

Me?

Girls like you, hellbent on conquering India and finding a husband. I remember them from my young days, lost but determined, their mouths set in grim tight lines. Some of them even stayed, though most came back empty-handed…

And you think I'm one of them?

Oh no, not you. The woman laughed and made to move

off. *My cabin's on G-Deck*, she said lowering her eyes knowingly. *If you ever get lonely.*

They had set her up with a room at the club that had no air-conditioning and she lay awake at nights watching the sluggish fan above her stirring the warm air around to no obvious purpose. There were film shows every Saturday, ponderous dramas that she has seen months before in Aberdeen, shown, here, by the poolside, with intervals between the reels when the men lumbered off to the bar to replenish their drinks and the women in their cotton dresses gathered in clusters to gossip.

George appeared about halfway through the performance, dressed in a clean pair of the white slacks that planters favoured and a brightly-coloured bush shirt patterned with leaping racehorses, his hair slicked back in a bold Brylcreem sweep. *Here we are then*, he whispered quietly as the floodlights dimmed and the film resumed. A banal Bob Hope comedy that had bored her even the first time she had seen it, though she could feel every woman's eyes on her in the hot and airless darkness.

They summoned me to head office this week, he said into her ear as Hope wisecracked his way out of some contrived situation. *They want us to set a date. Apparently although we're not the rulers here anymore we still need to set an example to the natives.*

She laughed, though it was an eerie hollow sound, and

then nodded. *The women are interviewing new servants for you even as we speak and apparently I'm being taken shopping for fabrics on Monday. It seems you've let your curtains and bedding go to rack and ruin and it's a disgrace to the British Empire.*

He smiled and put his arm around her, pulling her close, and she could smell sandalwood oil and medicated soap on his skin, unsuccessfully covering the lingering scent of the hot body which had reluctantly relinquished him from her bed not more than an hour before. *Will the end of the month suit you? The rains should have come by then and we can maybe breathe again…*

She shrugged. *I stopped breathing months ago,* she said more to herself than to anyone else. But he heard and understood.

agnes

Mother had closed her eyes for the last time under the gunmetal skies of a bleak November and not survived to see the dawn of the New Millennium, though, as potential disaster scenarios go, the predicted global fiasco had turned out to be pretty much of a damp squib. No aeroplanes had fallen from the sky, no computers had ceased to function. And, looking back on it, this rather sad little ceremony in the windswept island churchyard in the village where her parents had chosen to retire had ended up being the social highlight of Alison's year.

Attendance had been poor on the day, which had incensed her father, but those of her parents' friends who were still in possession of their mortal coils were mainly too far away in their respective mainland bungalows and had sent messages of condolence from their overstuffed suburban living rooms, their once hearty voices now soft and apologetic amidst their collections of neglected brassware and crumbling clay figurines. None of them, it seemed, possessed either the physical strength or the finances to make the long drive north and then catch one of the infrequent ferries to the island.

Your neighbours all came, she reassured her father as they walked slowly together from the graveside. *And all your*

19

old friends sent messages, she wasn't forgotten. It wasn't much comfort to him, she knew, but it was the best she had to offer as she took his cold hand in hers and led him to her car, the wind tearing at her hair, the sky leaden with an early dusk already descending.

It really was a good turnout, she assured him once again. *But I wish Agnes could have been here,* she added quietly, speaking only to herself, as she slid behind the wheel. *She would have wanted to attend…*

Agnes, resplendent in a new red and gold sari, stands stoically for the camera with a large Huntley and Palmer's biscuit tin containing Mother's cake for the Christmas party firmly under one arm. *Move about, Agnes,* Mother shouts from behind the camera. *It's a movie film.* She searches for the correct Hindi word. *Bioscope!* But Agnes stands firm, treating the viewer to her motionless profile, her raven hair tied neatly back, pale brown face expressionless except for the tight and determined set to her mouth.

The tiny stone-flagged main street is bustling with Saturday provisions-buyers and early Christmas shoppers, but they finally gain shelter from the November gales and manage to bag a table in the minuscule cafe attached to the island's Christian bookstore, and, sitting awkwardly across from her father amidst the clatter of dishes and incessant clean-cut singers warbling about Jesus, Alison suddenly asks: *You do remember Agnes, don't you, Dad?*

Agnes who? her father asks, blearily, like a sleeper awakening.

Agnes, her face immobile, sits cross-legged on the mosaic kitchen floor with a workaday cup of condensed-milk-sweetened tea in her hand. The other ayahs are lighting cigarettes or rolling betel leaves into neat cones while, next door, the mothers are taking a turn at supervising their own offspring, and the sound of little voices singing *Oranges and Lemons* can be heard even through the firmly closed door.

It is a mistake to become too fond of their children, Ayata, advises an old ayah in an unadorned widow's sari, her fat midriff bulging over the lower skirt. *Wash them, dress them, make sure they come to no harm, it is a fair exchange for what they pay us.*

Agnes says nothing. Daintily lighting a cigarette.

There is a quiet hour before bedtime when her parents are having their dinner that she spends nightly with Agnes, the two of them cross-legged on the cracked marble floor of the big bedroom that is really her playroom as, even in winter, it's too warm to sleep in, and she has a tiny bed -

almost a cot - in her parents room where there is air conditioning. Alison likes the scents of her ayah, neem soap and a faint trace of cigarette smoke, hair oil if you nuzzle against her neck and inhale. Tonight they are going thorough Mother's big alphabet book with its large garishly-coloured lithograph illustrations of apples and babies and English schoolboys in peaked caps symbolising each letter. It is a familiar tome and Alison is confident - far too confident for Agnes' liking - and she sing-songs her way through the letters until Agnes taps the book to indicate a required slowing of pace. The girl's kindergarten teacher is already impressed with her knowledge of letters and numbers and gives credit to her mother while Agnes stands stoically by their car in the red dust of the parking area, Alison's little blue-and-white-checked school case in her hand, clean socks in the car and a damp face flannel wrapped in plastic deep inside her copious hessian bag.

They drive home in the rapidly-descending dusk, the winter wind a banshee wail, flecks of snow in the air, the incoming tide angry and lashing at the rocky shore as the road perilously skirts the cliff tops then veers sharply inland under the watchful eyes of ancient standing stones.

That really is a dreadful cafe, Alison says, laughing, for want of something to break the silence between them as the car's headlamps pick out the sign for the single track road that will lead to her parents' little grey-stone cottage by the village church.

shame shames

Your mother always liked it, her father says shortly, and they travel the rest of the way to the tiny house in wordless animosity.

A parcel containing a heavy overcoat arrives from Home and the tailor comes to measure her for shirts and skirts while her mother is busy knitting a scarf. Agnes is very silent during these days, more silent than usual, and smells of cigarettes.

She stays with her father for four days after the funeral, helping him to ferry all of her mother's belongings to the incinerator - the old man being unable to bear the thought of donating anything to the charity shop and seeing some miscellaneous island woman dressed in his wife's clothing - and they pass the time together in almost perpetual silence, he refusing to accompany her to the ferry on the morning of her departure, and she drives through the dawn mist - the flat treeless landscape monochrome in the early light - to the pier and joins the desultory queue of cars waiting to board.

There seems to be an interminable delay getting a truckload of cattle aboard and she has secured her car in the lower hold and made her way to the upper observation deck before they finally cast off, and she watches the shore ebbing further and further into the miasma, the open sea a restless grey blanket, a swirling inverted cone of gulls following their progress out of the strait's relative calm. There is a fine spray of sleet in the air, and her face, almost numb with the cold, tastes of salt when she rubs her hand across it to wipe away a tear, realising that this will probably be the last time that she will see her father alive. The shock like two cold hands pressing down her lungs, her whole body shaking.

And at that moment she is that lonely six-year-old girl once more, standing on the deck of an ocean liner in the hot sun, brightly coloured streamers cascading into the air and tangling in the pure white foam of the ship's wake, the figure of Agnes, not waving or smiling, on the dockside getting smaller and smaller as they depart, and the sudden dawning that they will never, ever, hold each other again.

shadowlands

I t took just ten packing cases to ship all their possessions from India to the damp, almost windowless,
house that Edward had inherited, her whole history
encapsulated in half a score of wooden crates transposed
to a dark and unwelcoming abode down a sunless wynd
in a Scottish country town. All her surviving wedding
china, her mother's beloved canteen of silver cutlery, Father's framed watercolours, the hammered brassware that
she had collected over the years of her marriage, the skin
from the leopard that her brother had killed on a weekend
jaunt with his army chums, the endless clay figurines that
had decorated their dining room, her albums of photo-
graphs, Edward's eight-millimetre films in their yellow
Kodak bags and rusty metal tins, crumbling soapstone
models from visits to the Taj Mahal, hand-loom rugs,
silken hangings, ornaments ancient and modern, gifts sent
to her from long-dead relatives in Britain when Mother
had announced her engagement in *The Times*, her grandmother's tissue-thin bridal dress which she had worn to
her own wedding, the Aegean-blue Benares silk stole with
its gold embroidery that the Rajnapor Ladies Club had
presented to her as a farewell gift when Edward announced his retirement.

Mother had warned her against marrying a man more
than twenty years her senior but she had laughed at the

notion of spending her life with anyone else, but they had barely been in the new house a month - most of their worldly goods still crated up - when Edward complained of feeling unwell, went to bed early and never awoke, leaving her alone with the two girls in this bleak abode crammed full of their accumulated past, the staid furniture that had belonged to his mother draped in throws more suited to the hot azure light of sunnier climes.

A few neighbours had come to the funeral out of politeness, and an old woman, almost bent double, who introduced herself as a second cousin of Edward's, though the girls later reckoned that she was just some lonely old soul crashing the service in the hopes of a free meal later. The February weather was horrid, with sleety rain and a bitter wind whipping through the dark coat she had bought for the occasion, and - a fish out of water in this bleak province of the Northern Hemisphere - she could scarcely make out a word of the mumbled condolences that were muttered to her as mourners took their leave.

Her mother - a no-nonsense alderman's daughter from a Lancashire mill village - had boarded the steam packet from Liverpool to Bombay to marry the British subaltern she had been corresponding with for the last three years, and Elsie - born to the heat of the merciless sun and the lush monsoon greens of the rainy seasons - had known no other dwelling places than her father's white-pillared cantonment house and then the bougainvillea-draped bungalow in Rajnapor where she and Edward had settled and brought up their daughters.

Edward, on the other hand, sandy-haired and ruddy-cheeked, hailed from this very town - his family's names in the parish registers going back generations - first migrating to Dundee and the jute mills before taking his own long voyage across the ocean in the wake of the Great War, living a bachelor existence in Rajnapor for over a decade before he met her at a tennis *tamasha* - barely seventeen years old with her hair still in ringlets and her long tanned legs luscious in a short sports frock - and lost his heart; and now here she sat, a middle-aged widow in this strange, cold, grey-granite town with its sombre war memorial in the market square listing column after column of the dead, a very long way from home.

However, she told herself, she was here now and India was a long way away and - anyway - had become unwelcoming to her kind, so she decided that she had best put a brave face on it, slowly unpacking the beloved possessions designed for a different world, a different light, making the low-ceilinged rooms with their peeling smoke-stained wallpaper look even smaller and more cramped.

The years passed slowly and the girls grew older, no longer traipsing playing field mud over her silk rugs but, instead, staying out late and bringing home teenage magazines and gramophone records that she certainly didn't approve of, playing them loudly when she was not at home. The two of them, once so hellbent on living in her shadow, now preferring to watch sombre television plays about struggling young people in English slums when she dragged out the projector and wallowed in Edward's old films, marvelling at how young and carefree she had been in that lost world, almost skipping along the river embankment, the girls in their matching frocks and parasols being shepherded by their ayah in her wake; Edward and their friends sitting by the poolside with their drinks in their hands, ice cubes clinking, the skies and the water a breathtaking shade of brilliant blue. Everyone convinced that it could never possibly end.

Elizabeth was the first to formally rebel, and in the year that men landed on the moon her eldest daughter insisted on going to the art college in Dundee rather than taking the secretarial course that Elsie had picked out for her. Then, to make matters worse, Eva began attending dances with an unkempt young man who didn't appear to have any fixed employment, and her beautiful daughter now took to staying out until the wee small hours, coming home on unsteady feet, reeking of cigarette smoke and alcohol. Treating her mother's home like some cheap rooming house in a disreputable part of a distant city.

It was all too much to bear, and Elsie, forever a mapmaker, could watch her life, and that of her daughters, bumping forcibly off the path she had so meticulously plotted for them. Time, she reckoned, to take back the helm and steer the ship back to port, reconnect with her guiding star and navigate the dark waters to safety. Elizabeth was - surprisingly - the least of her worries, and at least progressing well at the art school and passing her exams. Eva, however, was running completely wild, and it was upon her wayward younger daughter that Elsie first turned her gaze. The root of the problem, she decided, was the feckless young man, his influence reaching deep below the surface like belladonna creeping into a well-tended garden and choking the life out of it, and Elsie went to the marble-pillared savings bank in the town square and withdrew one hundred and eighty pounds from her account, more than enough, she calculated, to make this particular weed disappear. And she was not wrong. Eva moped over his apparent defection for a few weeks then slowly began to see a lot of a man called Angus from the Farmer's Union offices, a few years her senior, it was true, but steady and dependable, and if Elsie had helped to set up meetings to encourage the match it was no more than a mother's duty, was it not?

Her role, she felt, was that of the puppet master when it came to her daughters' futures, and she remembered them constantly begging to be taken to the Artisans' Bazaar back in Rajnapor when they were little, that narrow canyon between tall buildings where the stallholders displayed their gaudy wares like a botanical garden in full bloom. Chinese fireworks, papier mâché masks, luxuriant floral garlands and khoi bags of all shapes and sizes bouncing in the breeze. Multi-propellored aeroplanes, majestic ocean liners, grinning cats, comic dogs, anthropomorphised moons and stars; the giant Bengal tiger they had splashed out on and bought for Elizabeth's fifth birthday party, and how she'd cried when Edward ruptured its belly and showered the children in puffed rice and four-anna plastic toys.

Hedonists by nature, the girls had been unimpressed by monkey men and dancing bears, and, on her fourth birthday, Eva had even wept for the fate of the poor animal in its tattered leather muzzle, its fur matted and its eyes dull, but they had both adored the shadow puppet theatres that nestled off the narrow bazaar lanes, clutching their rupee notes for admission like society women taking possession of their box at Covent Garden, enthralled at the oddly hypnotic scenes projected on the taut screens beyond the ragged velvet drapes salvaged from some long-departed memsahib's formal drawing room, the elephant-headed Ganesh, Krishna with his flute, epic stories of gods and goddesses acted out in song to the beat of a single drum, their ayah supplying details of the plots when their Hindi was stretched, their little faces rapt with awe.

Eva met her at the door when she returned from her walk, her normally neat hair wild and windswept by the February gales, roses in her cheeks. Spring was coming and there was still light in the sky, pink and purple like an old bruise, but her daughter had lit the living room fire and lighted the lamps.

I've been to see the doctor.

And?

And I'm pregnant.

Angus?

Don't be silly. There was a pause in which she could hear

all the clocks ticking and her own heart hammering, slowly rhythmically.

Oh... The other one.

A silence rose up between them and threatened to engulf them. A feeling like hate in the air, the taste of it cold and metallic in her mouth. Her daughter, her beautiful, beautiful daughter transformed into this sullen, steely-eyed woman with her arms folded tight against her thin chest. No trace left of that sunny little girl who had danced Ring-a-Ring-a-Rosies or wept salt tears for the fate of a bedraggled dancing bear. *I assume you've already decided what you want to do?*

The girl nodded. *I'll marry Angus, he's asked me more than once. We can live here. If you're amenable.*

As you wish. She walked past her without further comment and went slowly up the stairs, the rooms suddenly strange and filled with the paraphernalia of someone else's life, someone else's things. Edward was gone. The girls were all but gone too. The woman in the silk frock with the rich red rose pattern who had hosted parties on her palatial lawns with fleets of servants in attendance was likewise no more, like her little girls in their matching dresses and parasols, all of them fleeting shadows on the puppeteer's flickering screen.

She had no further use for this house, these objects, this ephemera from another life. Not bothering to remove her coat she pulled a small suitcase from the top of her wardrobe and packed a few things and went back down again. Eva was in the kitchen, furious as usual, banging pots and plates. There was no need for her to say anything further. Goodbyes were redundant.

the swimmer

for John Cheever

She had grown stout since having the children - the two of them less than a year apart - and now, not wishing to be seen unclad, she swam in the early morning when a fragile mist still lingered along the river embankment and the pool itself was as still as a mill pond. Even the shy Indian women who came coyly to the water's edge at breakfast time, still wrapped in their white saris, their long oiled hair unbraided, had not yet ventured from their restless beds, and Grace was alone save for the old Muslim *jummidar* with his net, creakily scooping up the fallen leaves from the spreading banyan tree on the hill leading up to the club house.

She liked to begin her morning swim by diving into the water from the pool's edge, breaking the surface's perfect skin like some Arctic creature plunging neatly through a thin membrane of ice, her big body suddenly graceful in the water like the great white seals that the sailors of her childhood storybooks mistook for mermaids, all those Nordic legends that she had planned on sharing with her own children before Morris had had his way and handed the two of them over to ayahs and feeding bottles before she could even hold them to her breast, both now shipped off to the same gruesome boarding school in Dorset that Morris himself had attended, spending their holidays with his sister in Bournemouth, polite letters on thin blue Aerograms once a fortnight with formal news of football matches and up-coming exams. Neither of them having the first idea of who she was.

Her head bursts out of the water in its old pale blue swimming cap, now sadly bereft of the bright rubber flowers that had originally adorned it when she first bought it in England, and she fills her lungs and begins to swim, a steady unremitting breaststroke, sixty-four lengths every morning - a mile each day if anyone was counting - briskly towelling herself down in the echoing cool of the marble-floored changing room before slipping a clean cinch-waisted frock over her head and going back to the bungalow in time for breakfast, approving the day's menus with the cook while Morris, waiting to be driven to his office in Calcutta, his clean white shirt already showing perspiration stains at the armpits, reads his *Times of India* over his customary morning repast of black tea and unbuttered toast, the thin sheets of newsprint like a confessional grid between them, as if he could no longer bear to even look at her, like the mosquito nets he still insisted on erecting over their separate beds at night.

Her days dragged once she had waved him off in the car, though he seldom even turned to acknowledge her valediction, and after a relatively short interview with the servants she settled down to read either the women's magazines that her sister had sent from London - the money-off coupons for lipstick or face powder all neatly clipped out - or the hefty leather-bound tomes from the club library: Kipling, Maugham, Rumer Godden, Pearl S Buck. All good colonial favourites which she had read several times over, but they passed the time of day until dinner and some stilted conversation with Morris before bed. The wife of a *kaaryaalay* sahib, she knew she was not particularly welcome among the other memsahibs and she preferred to leave them to their mahjong sessions and Caledonian Societies and keep her own company. They were polite enough when they met her, of course - though she knew that they called her Fatty Fredricks behind her back - but their menfolk were openly hostile to Morris, having no time for this cold-blooded Englishman from Head Office with his minor public school accent and fastidious ways. Morris Minor they all called him, even to his face.

It was only in the pool where she felt truly alive, and she treasured her hour of solitude each morning as she swam length after length, her heavy arms strong and able, her legs kicking like pistons, moving silently through the water with hardly a ripple, her breathing steady, her heart pumping, every fibre of her being scintillating as the sun rose steadily in the east, burning off the ephemeral river mist and bleaching the indigo of the dawn sky to a blinding white.

She undressed quickly in anticipation of the water's first chill, wearing her swimsuit under yesterday's frock, a clean outfit and underthings stowed in her bag along with her hairbrush and towel, rapidly pulling the dress up over her head and kicking off her sandals, often not bothering to close the cubicle curtain in the cool privacy of the ladies' changing rooms, anxious to be in the water and escape the quiet desperation of her day to day life. And yet... And yet today felt somehow different, the morning out of sorts, a feeling of something out of kilter, something amiss, and as she walked gingerly out to the poolside, the concrete paving slabs already hot underfoot, she saw him on the highest diving board, tall and white, sailing into the sky like an airborne swan.

He seemed to hover midair for a long second, then he cut through the static blue of the water like a keenly-sharpened blade and broke into an easy crawl, length after length without pause, back and forward, back and forward, while she stood mesmerised on the side, bitterly resenting this alien intrusion and yet fascinated by him simultaneously, seeing him as both an intruder and a kindred spirit, resented and yet more than welcome. The personification of the dark and secret things that she fantasised about during the hot and sleepless pre-monsoon nights.

Are you not coming in? he called to her now, smiling pleasantly as he flipped in the water like some ocean-born thing, selkie, shape-shifter, demon lover of the deep. His body long and white. Practically hairless save for his thick brown locks, the skin on his arms freckling, his shoulders going red and starting to peel from exposure to an unaccustomed sun. His accent Scottish though cultured - Edinburgh maybe - not at all like the harsher mill-worker's tones of the other Scots here. His features fine and even. Limbs long and athletic, a trained swimmer, maybe even

a rower, she thought as he spanned the pool effortlessly
and came back like a sailing ship on the evening tide. *I
don't bite,* he teased, laughing at her reticence, though not
unkindly.

For God's sake, don't just stand there like an idiot, Grace, she
whispered to herself, and, pausing until he had his back to
her and was nearing the far end of the pool, she dived
quickly into the water at the opposite side, at once feeling
to be a part of him, like two embryo twins sharing the
same womb, the same life-giving fluids. *Finally, someone
who makes me feel alive,* a voice somewhere deep inside her
suddenly whispered as her head broke the surface of the
water and she began to swim, castigating herself for this
adolescent foolishness as she counted length after length,
ignoring him but simultaneously absorbing him, feeding
from the aura he was leaving in the water, the wake from
him like an invisible phosphorescence when he heaved
himself out like a white streak - spurning the aid of the
ladder - and strode off nonchalantly towards the changing rooms. Whistling, by God. Leaving her to the solitude that she so craved yet - today - no longer cared for.
God *damn* this boy and his carefree arrogance.

He was there again the next day and the next, and on the
Thursday he arrived well before her and climbed out and
lay dripping on the grass by the men's changing room as
she went into the ladies' to undress, letting the sun dry his
long body while she swam, the whiteness that had so fascinated her when she first saw him turning now to a deep

golden brown, his arms a veritable sea of freckles. The already hot sun drying his bathing costume so that it clung to his body and outlined everything so clearly that he might as well have been lying there naked, showing it off. God damn him.

She swam quickly and without pleasure, not completing her normal quota of lengths and leaving early while he still lay there, feigning sleep, drying herself so violently that the towel hurt her skin, and she was curt to Morris and raised her voice to the cook when she got home, spending the whole day agitated and annoyed, finally retreating to the bathroom in the hottest part of the afternoon and lying soaking in the huge marble tub, her eyes squeezed tightly shut, touching herself under the water in a way that she had never done since she was a teenager.

Her sister had insisted on going to art school to study fashion, and was now a senior buyer for a small London mail order company, but Grace had remained quietly at home in Poole and gone instead to secretarial college, quickly mastering the mysteries of Pitman and securing a well-paid job in a local office while her sister struggled on her grant, speedily climbing the ladder and ending up as personal secretary to Morris, then a shy but particular man who seldom conversed but who had unexpectedly proposed marriage to her when he received the news of his posting to Rajnapor, and she had spent their short but very chaste engagement fantasising about the exotic life in India which awaited her, though uncomfortably aware that Morris had never expected her to oblige him as all the previous men in her life had done.

She casually asked the club bearers about the boy on the Friday when they came down to open up the pool bar at eleven, and learned that he was the nephew of Hugh McGregor - a fiery-tempered Scottish bachelor who hated Morris with a passion - and that he was here for a few weeks' holiday before returning to the varsity at St Andrews in the autumn. *He will study to be a famous doctor and perhaps will come back to India to tend to the starving poor,* they joked, and she could see him in his duffle coat, text books under his arm, a light dusting of snow in his hair against a pewter November sky; or at a concert in the ruins of the abbey in the early spring, nonchalant in his maroon gown, flirting effortlessly with middle-aged American ladies in town for the golf. She hated the very sight of him. And simultaneously desired him.

She continued to see him in the pool each morning but stayed aloof and now barely exchanged more than a few words with him beyond good morning, though her mind raged with scenarios that became more and more lurid as she swam calmly through the shimmering blue water, matching him length for length, her countenance calm, her body in turmoil. In a favourite fantasy she visualised workmen beginning repairs to the changing rooms and leaving the ladies' and gents' chambers separated only by a heavy hessian curtain. Suddenly, in a fit of violent passion, he would pull the drapes to one side and come upon her drying herself, her big body an arctic white where her swimsuit would have been, her arms, legs and shoulders burnt nut brown, her breasts and torso as pallid as her whole body had been when she took that fateful train journey to Liverpool and boarded the Anchor Line ship that brought her to the sub-continent. Or, in a bolder mood, she would sometimes even visualise herself slipping shyly through the recently opened doorway and finding him naked in the shower, his expression indifferent to her presence but his lower body giving away his obvious arousal.

Thus tortured, her days became feverish and blurred, and though she still retreated to her magazines each morning, her concentration faltered in the raging heat of the afternoons; dreading every breathless night when the sky crackled with wildfire lightning until the end of May when the rains would finally come, turning the once-tranquil blue waters of the pool to a deep and threatening green, its normal glass-like surface now a boiling cauldron in which they would both swim regardless.

Then, just as unexpectedly as he had first exploded into her life, he was gone, and one calm morning in early August she found herself alone again, the still waters of the pool returned to her as she swam and swam and swam, seeing for the first time her whole future stretching out before her in the lengths and miles of water ahead which would eventually, if added together, have taken her safely home and left this empty, soulless life far, far behind her.

the rains

When the rains came the river ran high, and often, after a heavy shower, the garden flooded and tangled wreaths of water hyacinth and sometimes the drowned bodies of small animals washed up and lay rotting on her grass in the early morning sun. Nothing large, thank God, although she had sometimes seen the bloated corpses of cattle floating down the middle of the torrent, white-bibbed vultures perched nonchalantly upon them, leisurely pecking, like obese diners on a down-at-heel liner.

Their bungalow, with its turmeric-yellow-washed walls, sagging green shutters and leaky tiled roof, had originally been a whites-only boarding house run by the wife of a Scot who had perished in the relief of Burma, but - as the main expat tourist trade all flocked to Simla or Darjeeling in the hot months - this far up-river from Calcutta there were only army subalterns or relatives of Rajnapor jute wallahs, and you could never charge top dollar for rentals, so Gilbert got the place for a relatively good price - dodgy roof and all - when the widow finally packed her bags and headed back to Coupar Angus.

Shirley sighed and shifted in her chair, her book abandoned on the rickety bamboo table beside her. She could still see their old house on the hill across the river, its white-pillared portico defiantly stark against the skyline and looking like a misplaced Tara from Mother's beloved *Gone With the Wind*, its bloated pomposity glaring down contemptuously at the mill compound below, the storm-battered iron jetty bustling with stevedores loading and unloading wagons on the private railway that Father's company had built for the original British factory owners long before Partition, importing the two sturdy locomotives from Sheffield and laying the track themselves from native metal, the sturdy little engines still chugging along their courses as the cranes lifted the heavy bales of raw jute from the procession of down-at-heel river barges that queued with their wares.

They had had a whole fleet of servants back in those days, two cooks, over fifteen *maalees*, three bearers, separate ayahs for herself and Gilbert, sweepers, washerwomen, the whole complement. Now they only had old Abdul who had been adopted by Mother as a boy of fifteen when Gilbert was just a toddler, before Shirley was even born; and Gilbert had just celebrated his sixty-fifth birthday before the rains came, so heaven knows how old Abdul was now, though he was still alert and upright, presiding stiffly over dinner each night in his starched white uniform, even though they all knew that there was no cook and that he had prepared their meal himself.

Of course, after Gilbert won his court case everything would be grand again, their old house restored to them, the disputed dividends from the company paid directly to Gilbert's account, and their old aunt back in Scotland had even promised them her farmhouse in her will if they ever wanted to go back Home to retire. She smiled at that. The newspapers were always full of stories about the Americans and the Russians racing each other to put men onto the moon, yet she had never been further than Calcutta in her entire life. It was a funny old world.

She heard a faint rumble of thunder and looked up at the lowering sky and sighed again, rising stiffly from her wicker chair on the veranda and walking slowly into the house to change her dress and help Abdul prepare tea. It was a court day and Gilbert would be back from Calcutta soon, worn out but full of good news of how the case was progressing, hungry for the tiny lady-like sandwiches that Abdul was so adept at making, slicing the cucumber so thinly that it was almost transparent, then storing the platter under a damp cloth in the ice box so that the butter wouldn't go rancid in the stormy heat.

She adored the way that Gilbert looked on court days, so dashing, even at this age, in his navy suit and pale chambray shirt combined with Father's regimental tie and a powder blue silk handkerchief in the breast pocket. He had never served in the army himself, of course, on account of his bad leg, and even as a young man had walked with a cane, but it had never stopped all her girlfriends swooning over him when he arrived in Calcutta on a rare day's holiday and came to her boarding school to take her to lunch at Firpo's or Trinca's, all of them angling to be asked along, though he never did, cherishing his ephemeral freedom from the rigours of the railway company and wanting to have her all to himself for their brief time together.

43

Passing the open front door, she could hear the approaching train whistle, just as the clouds burst and a torrential monsoon shower began to teem down, pitting the river surface and pounding on the roof like a deranged drummer as she hurriedly called for Abdul to check the buckets in the attic, though, as usual, he was already ahead of her, stiffly ascending the treacherous ladder as the torrent commenced to batter down on the sun-cracked tiles and streams of water began to drip down everywhere. They would, of course, repair the roof as soon as the case was won, Gilbert had promised. It would be their top priority. *Meanwhile, it's no trouble for you and Abdul to place a bucket or two up in the loft, is it, Pigeon? I'd help, of course, but it's a bit of a kerfuffle with the old leg and all that.*

Damn, damn, damn this weather! Now Gilbert's suit would get all muddy and she's have to send Abdul into Calcutta to get it cleaned as Gilbert would never tolerate the local dhobie touching it. Heavens, he complained enough about how his shirts and handkerchiefs were ironed as it was, and, of course, he needed to look his best in court, but this would mean at least an extra ten rupees out of her scant housekeeping allowance. Damn and blast this *blasted* rain.

She could see him now, cursing loudly, flapping along the road like a bad-tempered goose, his cane thrashing ahead of him in pique, one carefully manicured hand holding the powder blue handkerchief girlishly above his head, his suit already drenched, the trouser legs soaking and mud-splattered, his shirt sticking to his skin; and she ran heedlessly out of the house and into the downpour to meet him, uselessly holding her umbrella over him for the last few paces as she helped him up the front veranda steps and into the shelter of their home.

The rain had stopped while they were at tea and given way to a steamy late afternoon sun which quickly evaporated all the puddles in the rutted roadway to their house, leaving the banana trees and thick vegetation that encircled them on the land side of the river lush and verdant; but by the time Abdul had cleared away dinner dishes the skies had opened again and there was an unrelenting curtain of water cascading down outside as she carefully measured out that evening's ration of kerosene and lit the lamp in the lounge, settling down beside Gilbert on the battered leather sofa that had come from Father's study in the big house and running her hands through his thick silver hair, worn, as always, unfashionably long, as he laid his head in her lap and let her cosset him. He had changed into the red silk kimono that Mother had brought back from her honeymoon in Japan, forsaking the more formal robe which he wore with a yellow cravat in the colder months, having regaled her with endless tales of Carmichael, their lawyer, cutting the attorneys of the railway company down to the quick and casting their objections to one side, the judge, he thought, almost ready to rule in their favour. *Yes, Pigeon, just you wait, we'll be back in our old house before you know it and living the life of Riley once more.*

She nodded and continued her caresses, feeling his head

grow heavier as he slowly fell into a deep, child-like slumber, his breathing regular, his features losing their permanent worried frown and becoming again that fey little boy who had led such a carefree existence in a world which had ceased to exist decades before. Father had never liked him, of course, but had duly put him to work in the railway company at sixteen and had insisted that the new owners keep Gilbert on when he sold them his holdings, though when the old man died the shrewd Marwari bosses saw no reason to keep paying a salary to a superfluous white man who did little or nothing all day; not to mention occupying - rent free - the domestic property which they had also purchased, and she had quietly given Gilbert her own savings to purchase the down-at-heel bungalow where they now resided, all the servants bar Abdul deserting them as soon as the news of their financial situation became public. And, God knows, it was well over a year since even that poor man had been paid any wages, surviving as he did on a small charpoy in his room at the rear of the house and the leftovers from the meals which he prepared for their table.

Carmichael, she knew, had cruelly dismissed Gilbert's histrionic claims of unfair dismissal as hopeless on their first interview, but Abdul dutifully packed sandwiches and that day's newspaper into a briefcase once a week for her brother's court trip to Calcutta, where he sat in the cool of the corridors all day reading his paper, sometimes prevailing on the few old friends of Father's who remained to treat him to morning tea or even lunch, eating his now-stale sandwiches on the slow train journey home, dabbing at his nose with a cologne-soaked handkerchief as he was jostled along in the third class compartment.

And they stayed, really, because they had no money and nowhere else to go. The aunt in Scotland had been dead for years, her 'farmhouse' a pitiful ruin which had been condemned and pulled down by the local authority, the old lady herself deemed an imbecile who had ended her days in the asylum; and one day Abdul would also die quietly, she knew, still proudly wearing his starched white bearer's uniform and black Jinnah cap, and Gilbert would fade away soon after, bereft without his faithful friend, both of them leaving her alone in this falling down shanty of a house until she too met her maker, no doubt lying rotting on Mother's Japanese silk rug and food for all the geckos and cockroaches who lived in the cracked plaster of the walls, her remains discovered months later by some passing pedlar who would leave her there without prayer or blessing.

max scratchmann

skip, lilac, skip

The stiff ballerina's net of her costume was brittle and unyielding, crackling with static as she moved, the too tight bodice chaffing her underarms, the clumsy headdress threatening to cover her eyes and make her trip when she skipped. And, as if having to play the Lilac Fairy wasn't bad enough at her age, the concert had been rescheduled at the last minute and now all the Loretto boarders were home from Darjeeling and were going to be in the audience to witness her humiliation, and - even worse - would promptly relay it to everyone at the school when she went up after the Christmas holidays.

She had begged, no, *pleaded,* with Miss Robbie to do something different from Dance of the Flower Fairies, even taking in the book of Enid Blyton children's plays that her Gran had sent on her last birthday, and pointed out the story about the motherless brothers and sisters who have to look after their home while their father seeks work as a gardener, but the old lady had merely tutted, the powder quivering on the stiff hair of her upper lip, and dismissed the whole idea out of hand. Stating that they had no boys to play the father or big brother's parts when pressed. Though she'd had no problem with getting girls to play boy's parts when they'd done that awful pantomime last year, and Caroline was still living down her humiliation at having to play Buttons to Joanna MacDonald's club-footed

49

Cinderella at that particular fiasco.

Her mother's Caledonian Society friends used to whisper that Miss Robbie had come to India years before to find a husband and lodged with her bachelor army brother while she searched. The search having been fruitless and the brother having eventually departed at Partition, she had been taken pity on by the Sisters in the convent and employed to give English lessons to the poor Indian children who attended the nuns' shanty of a school five miles upriver, receiving only her bed and board as remuneration, and she scraped a meagre crust by producing plays and concerts for the rapidly dwindling coterie of British children still active on the palatial mill compounds. Though there were already three Indian girls in the play this Christmas, though all the Memsahibs were all pretending not to notice.

Caroline sighed and looked at herself in the changing room mirror, ears too big, face too round and pink, her chubby neck a nasty shade of red where the costume was rubbing. And, of course, her chest, well, that was still as flat as a pancake, not a sign of anything happening there, even though she was twelve and a quarter and a whole five months and eleven days older than Joanna MacDonald who was always showing off the two poached eggs in her vest as if they were the biggest things to land on the planet since Marilyn Monroe.

We're waiting for you, Lilac, Miss Robbie's voice floated up from the stage, trying to sound soft and motherly but not quite masking the edge of irritation that Caroline always inspired in her. Thank God she was going to board at Loretto after the holidays, or, at least that's where she hoped she was going.

Would we not be better just sending her to school in Edinburgh? her mother had reasoned to Dad when she didn't know that Caroline was eavesdropping. *Heaven knows what's going to happen here when the bloody Marwaris take over? They'll shut the club, that's for sure, and the pool. And it's only a matter of time before the blasted government kicks us all out anyway. And it would just be the one plane ticket we'd have to find the money for, she could stay with your sister in the holidays...*

Edinburgh. She dimly remembered it from her father's last home leave. They had gone one foggy day in late October to visit an old aunt of her mother's in Marchmont, a tiny fire in the grate, the house cold and dusty with half-empty rooms echoing like a derelict museum, tableaux of dead birds arranged under glass domes everywhere, their feathers dyed to simulate brightness but not succeeding. The little square of frost-kissed lawn outside where she had been sent to play while the adults drank tea, the thin yellowed grass surrounded by wilting fuchsia bushes - Kilties, her great aunt called them - the blooms withered and dying back, the stems drooping. Then she had been taken to the zoo, the afternoon light already fading, the animals cowed and huddled into the corners of their cages, the whole place making her want to cry, an unearthly quiet to a quarter that should have been filled with colour and sound, nothing at all like the bustle of the Calcutta menagerie, with the shrieks of baboons and roars of

51

tigers in descant with the competing cries of popsicle vendors and pakora sellers.

Then, finally, High Tea at Jenners before Waverley and the train back to Dundee; the now dark street crowded with late shoppers and people scurrying home from work, Christmas lights garlanded in mistletoe-like clusters from the shops to the gardens, nothing switched on yet until some ceremony involving the Lord Provost took place nearer Yuletide, trams trundling past, packed to the gunwales, a scent of sulphurous energy in the air as they sparked from their power cables, like the wildfire lightning in the air at home in the hot weeks before the monsoon broke. Then, suddenly, a lull in the clatter and the sound of a drunk woman's voice, clear as a bell, singing Rudolph the Red-Nosed Reindeer into the frosty night air, before a motor bus turned in from one of the side roads and broke the stillness once more.

Caroline, get down here! Now! Miss Robbie barked up the three short steps that led to the dressing room, and, sighing, she trudged heavily down to meet her fate. *Now remember, girls, and particularly you, Caroline,* the old lady commanded as she took her seat at the piano. *Light on your feet and Skip!*

Your neck's all red, Joanna MacDonald smirked as Miss Robbie thumped out the opening chords of their dance and Caroline looked out into the audience at her mother and her friends all in their best peony-print frocks, her dad at the back of the hall, still in his white mill clothes. Fat Mr Fredricks from head office in the front row, the only man in the audience wearing a tie, already looking bored but determined to assert his authority on the gathering. And then she saw the row after row of beautiful Indian mothers in their best saris, hair glistening with coconut oil and bejewelled with gold and tiny rubies, their faces rapt, like a flock of tame peacocks in their auric-threaded hues of sapphire and azure.

And suddenly she knew that she would not go to Loretto after the holidays, that her family's days here were numbered and that she and her kind were the last guests at a party where they had already long-overstayed their welcome. The sound of monsoon rain on the river or the crackling night skies of late May were not to be the symphonies that she would grow to womanhood to, and her lot was in the sleet and rain of a Scottish winter, the dark nights and foggy wynds of Strathmartine, the hushed voices of old ladies after the Kirk on a Sunday afternoon and the scents of plucked daffodils in springtime blending with the subtle aroma of mothballs from her grandmother's best fur coat.

Joanna MacDonald heard her cue and galumphed onto the stage in the ridiculous rose costume that her mother had insisted on making for her, as Caroline felt her best friend, Manjula, gently take her hand.

Are you ready to go? Manjula whispered, her familiar scent a mixture of sandalwood oil and neem soap, her breath like a warm summer breeze in Caroline's ear.

Y*es,* Caroline whispered back. *Let's skip*

max scratchmann

glossary

ayah: Children's nanny

charpoy: A native Indian bed, usually a wood frame with a string lattice

jummidar: Sweeper

kaaryaalay sahib: A senior official, an office worker, one who does not get his hands dirty.

khoi bags: Piñatas. Colourful figures made of paper and filled with puffed rice and cheap toys for children to scramble for at parties.

maalees: gardeners

Marwaries: Wealthy Indian business men.

Memsahib or Burrah Memsahib: A European lady, or the head European lady in a particular community

paan: Beetle-nut leaves dabbed with spices and folded into a cone

sindura: The red spot a Hindu man wears on his forehead

tamasha: A garden party or function

max scratchmann

shame shames

also by max scratchmann

Memoir

The Last Burrah Sahibs
Scotland for Beginners
Chucking It All

Short Fiction

Bad Girls
Mermaids in a Jar

max scratchmann